Marvel Ultimate Spider-Man

DOOMED!

ADAPTED BY Nachie Castro

Based on the animated series Marvel's *Ultimate Spider-Man*

YO, NOVA!
DOESN'T THAT ARMOR GET KINDA STINKY AFTER A WHILE?

Marvel Universe on Disney XD

Marvel
marvelkids.com

Printed in the United States of America

First Edition

1 3 5 7 9 10 8 6 4 2

G658-7729-4-12335

ISBN 978-1-4231-5474-7

Sustainable Forestry Initiative
Certified Chain of Custody
Promoting Sustainable Forestry
www.sfiprogram.org
SFI-01415
The SFI label applies to the text stock

IGNORE HIM AND TURN THE PAGE!

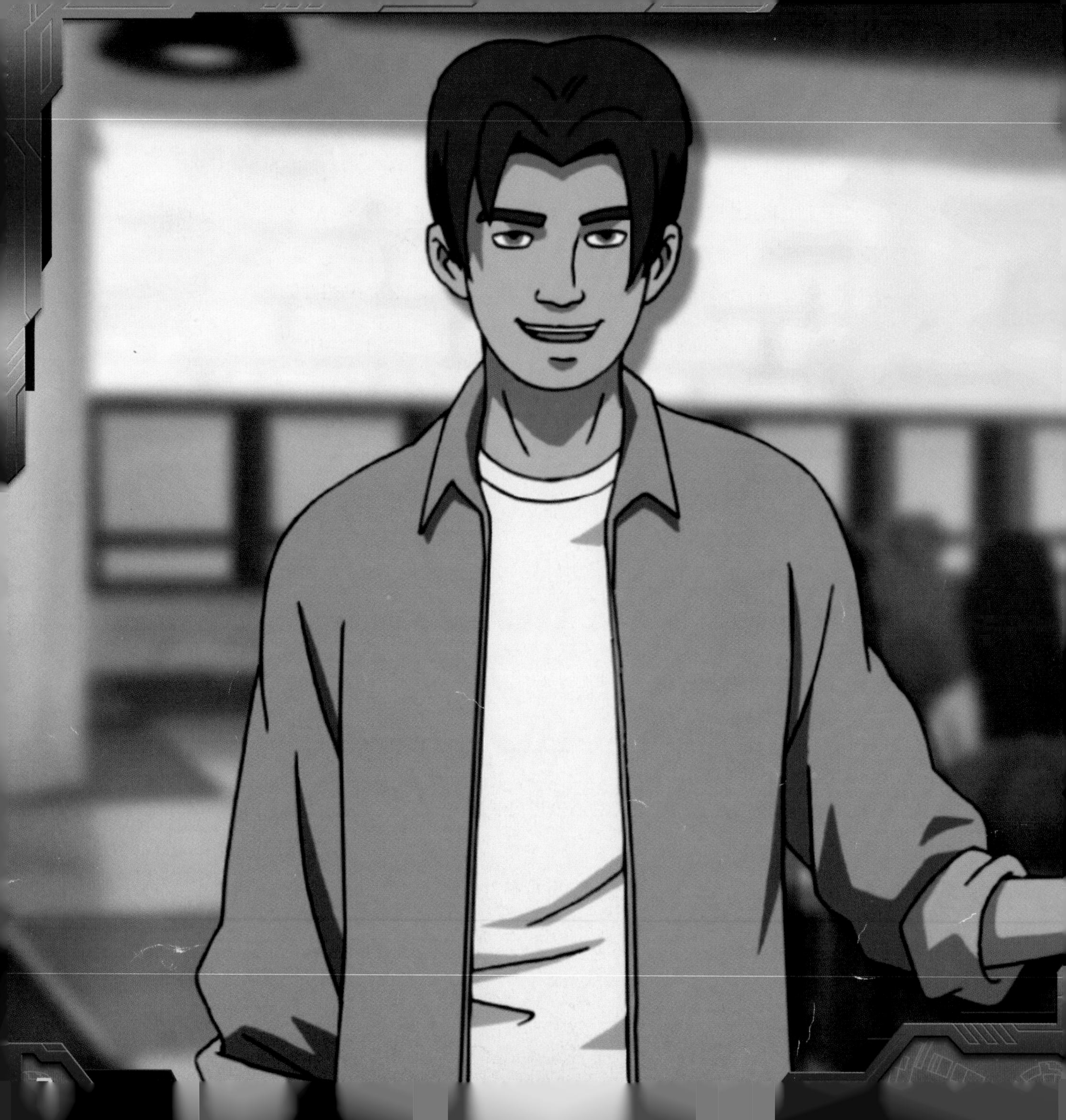

Peter Parker's life had been turned upside-down when Nick Fury, super spy and leader of S.H.I.E.L.D., had offered to help him become the Ultimate Spider-Man. Now Spidey wasn't just fighting bad guys, he was learning how to save the world!

But he wasn't alone. Nova, White Tiger, Power Man, and Iron Fist were there to help!

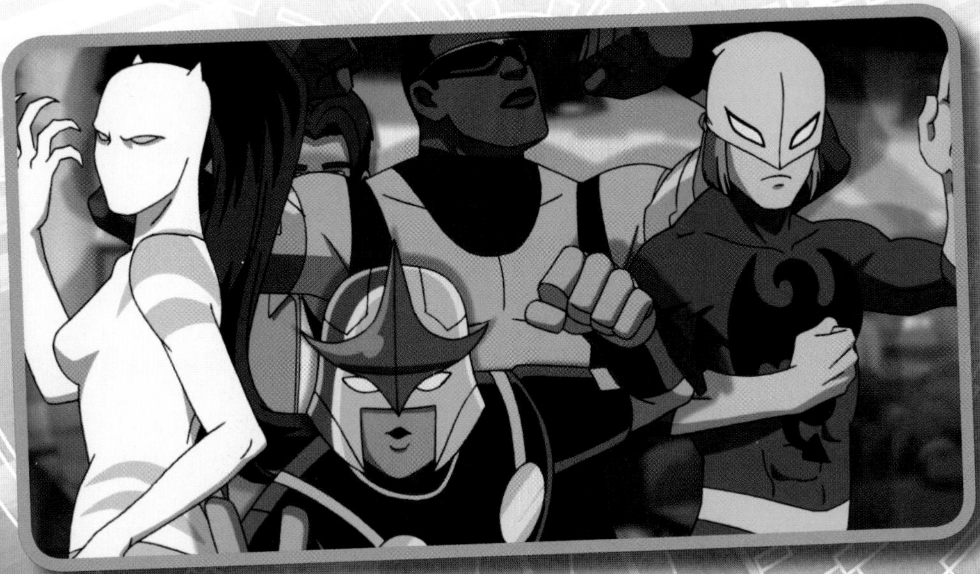

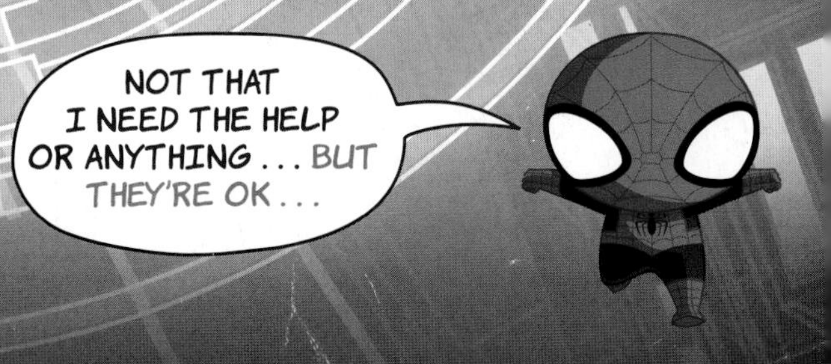
NOT THAT I NEED THE HELP OR ANYTHING . . . BUT THEY'RE OK . . .

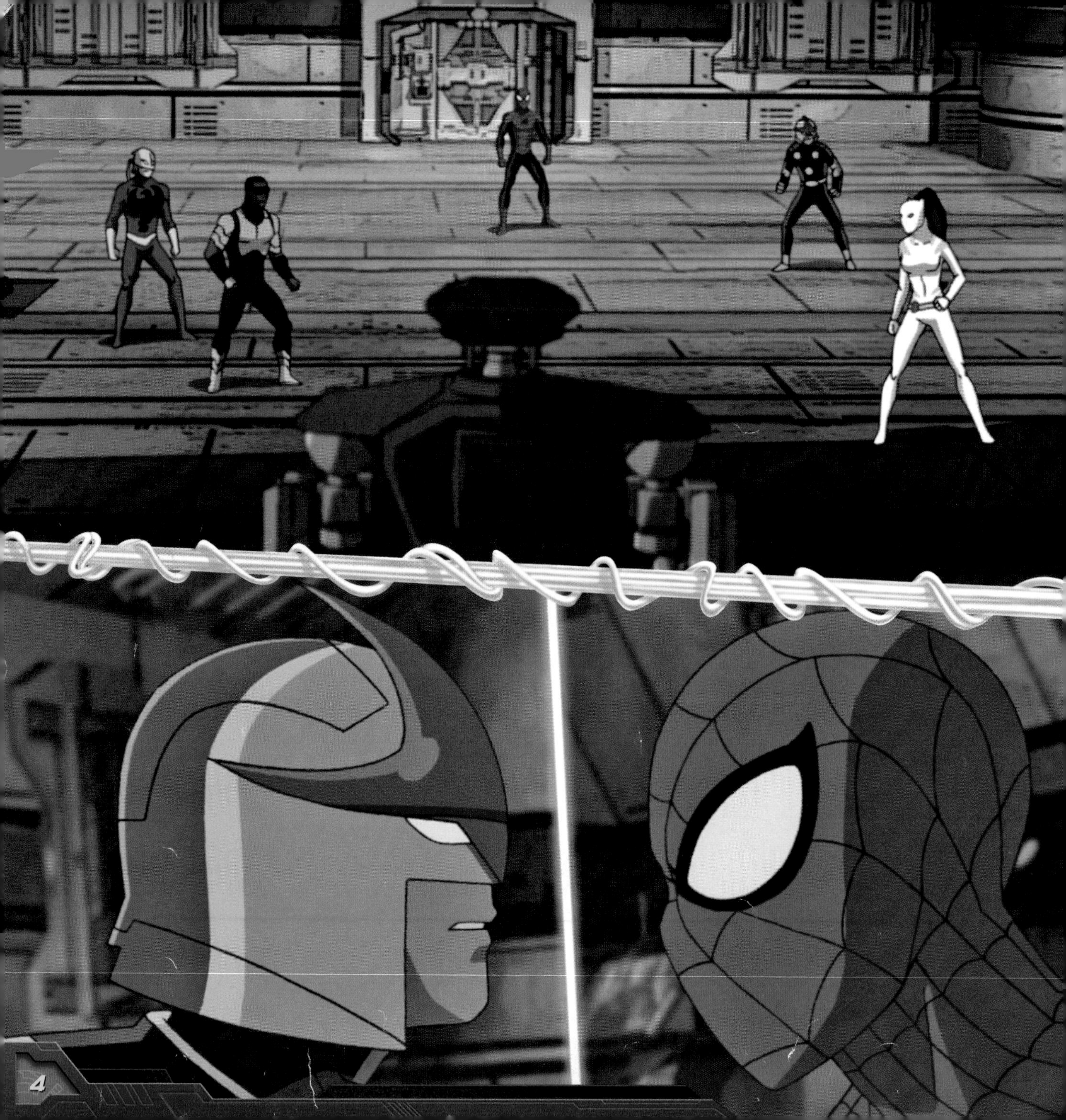

Fury had the new super team brought to a secret training facility in his headquarters, the gigantic Helicarrier.

After Spider-Man and Nova managed to spectacularly fail a test from Fury, they decided to prove they were ready for some real responsibility. Nova thought the best way to prove they were real Super Heroes would be to take down the baddest Super Villain in the world: Dr. Doom!

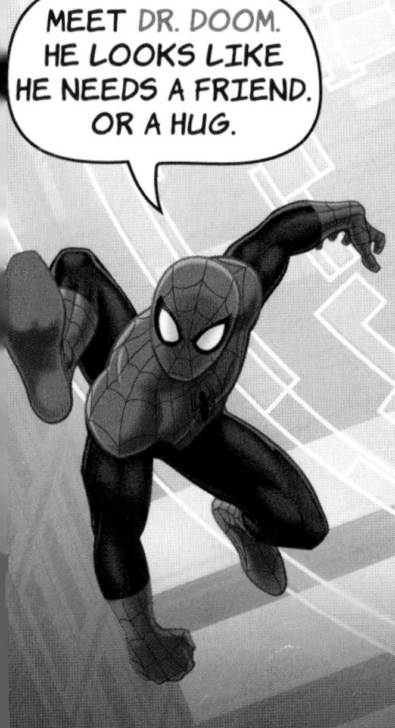
MEET DR. DOOM. HE LOOKS LIKE HE NEEDS A FRIEND. OR A HUG.

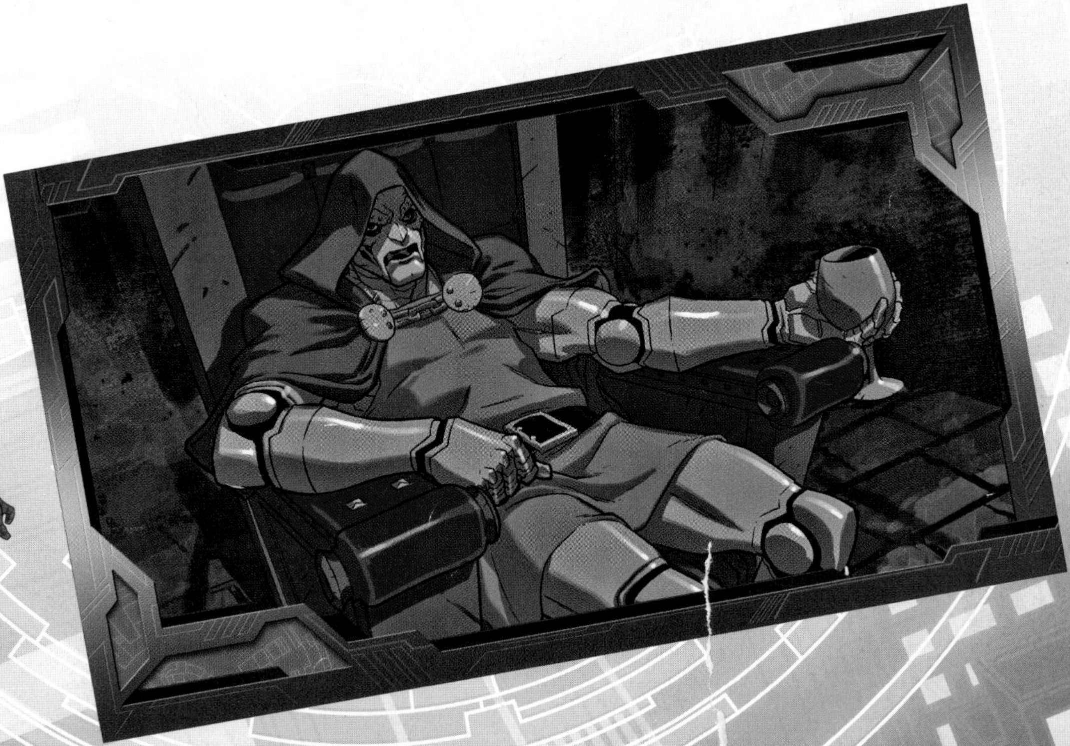

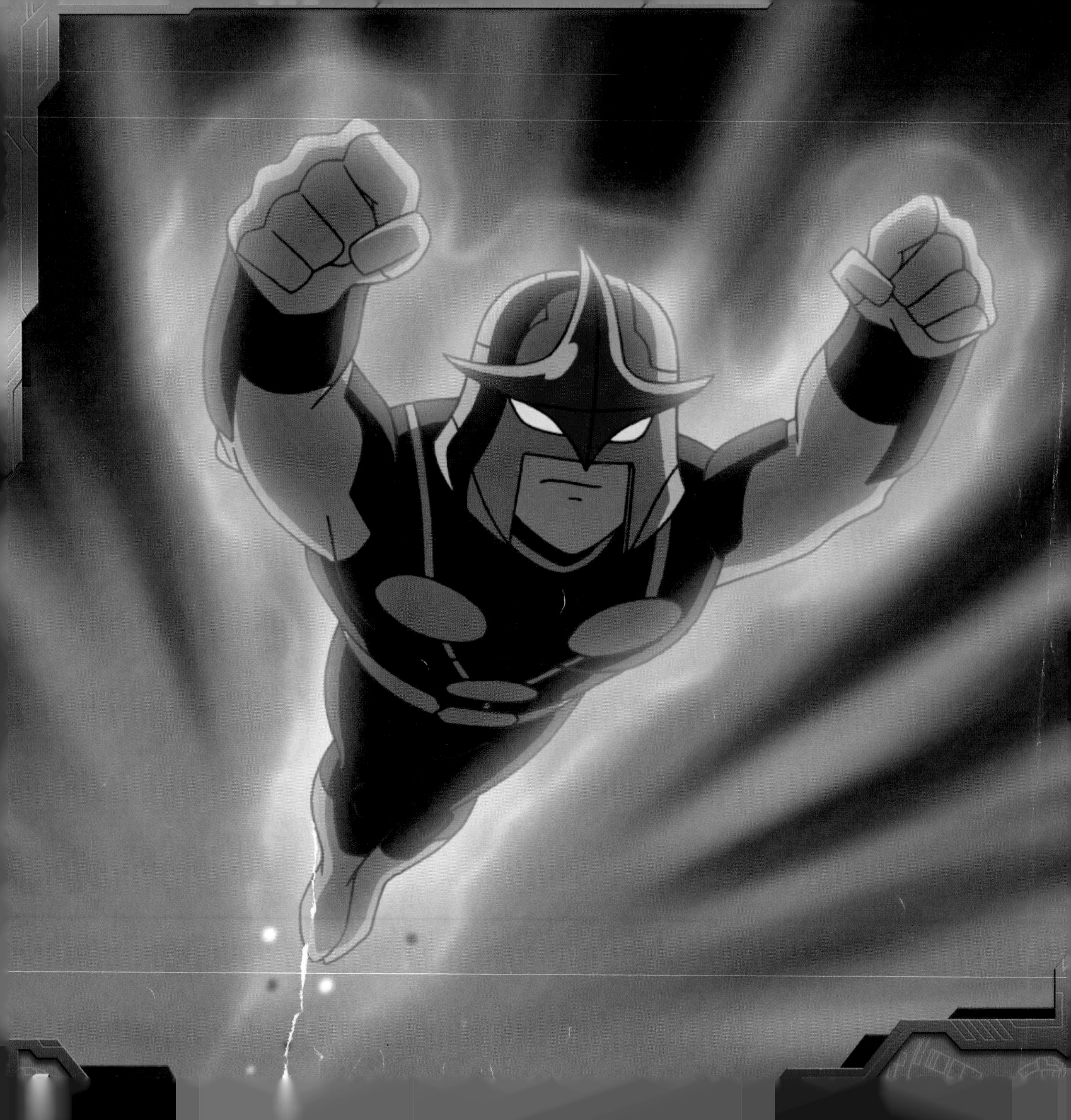

The team flew to Doom's homeland of Latveria in a S.H.I.E.L.D. jet. "Do we have a plan?" asked Power Man.

Spidey nodded. "I was gonna go up to the castle and say: 'Cupcake-gram!' Everyone loves cupcakes". White Tiger just shook her head. Children, she thought.

Once they were close enough, Nova took off to take on Doom's forces! "There's nothing you can build that I can't break!" Nova said, flying into action against rockets and robots.

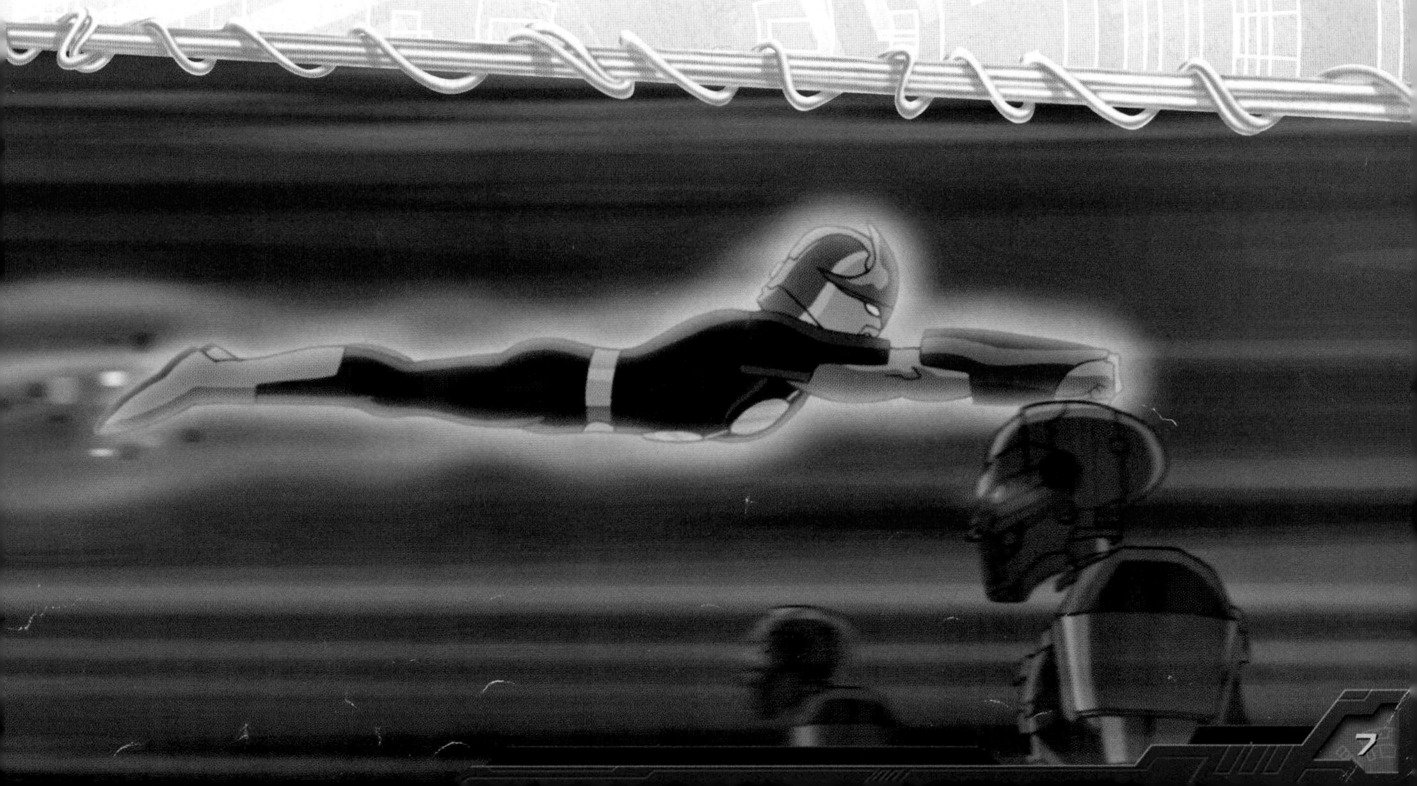

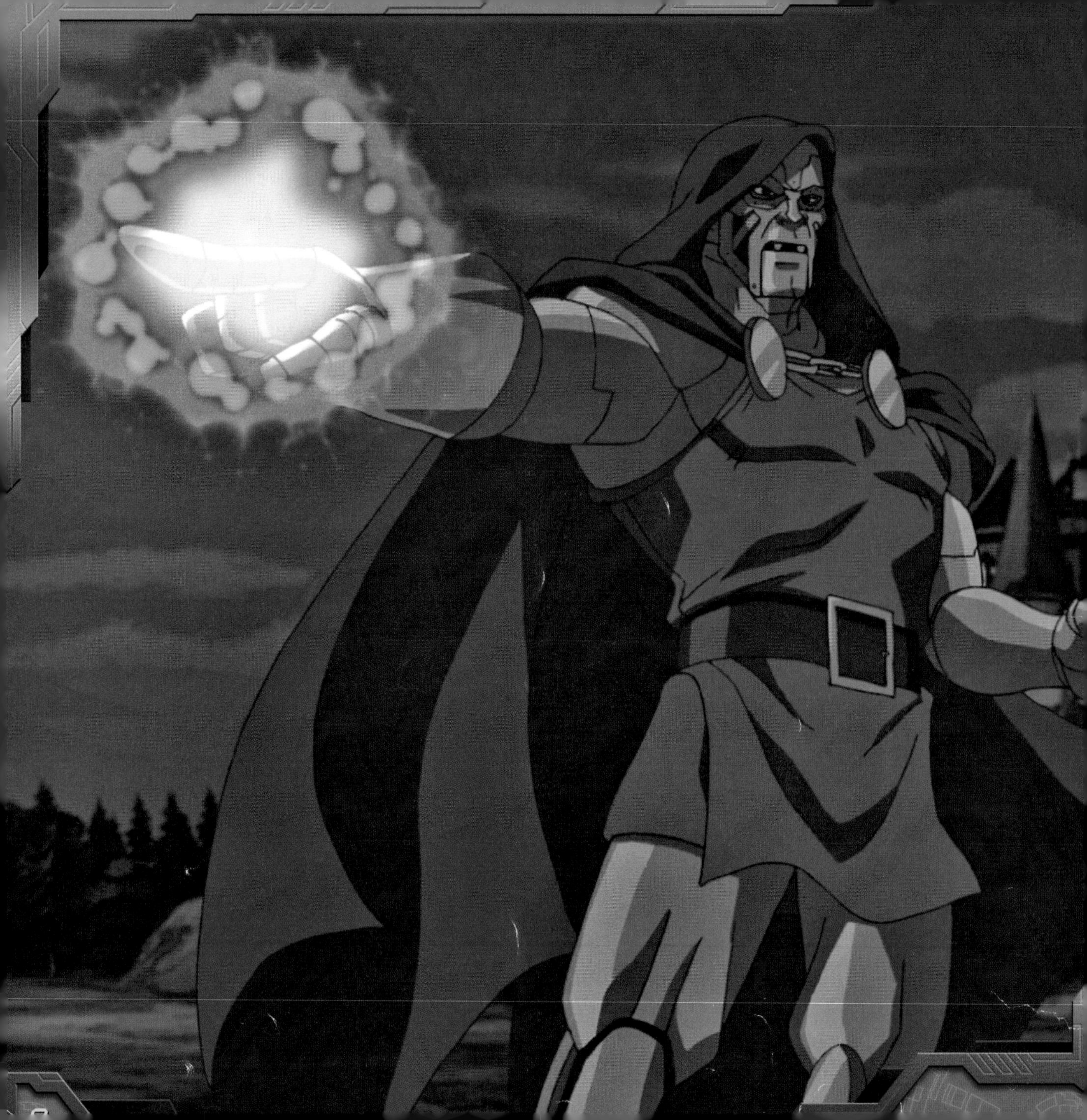

Nova took on the heavy artillery while Spider-Man and the rest of the team fought Doom's robot guards. It looked like Nova's crazy plan was going to work!

. . . until Dr. Doom himself joined the party.

"Look upon me, and tremble," a deep voice boomed from the night sky. A chill ran down the spine of each of the teenage heroes as Doom appeared!

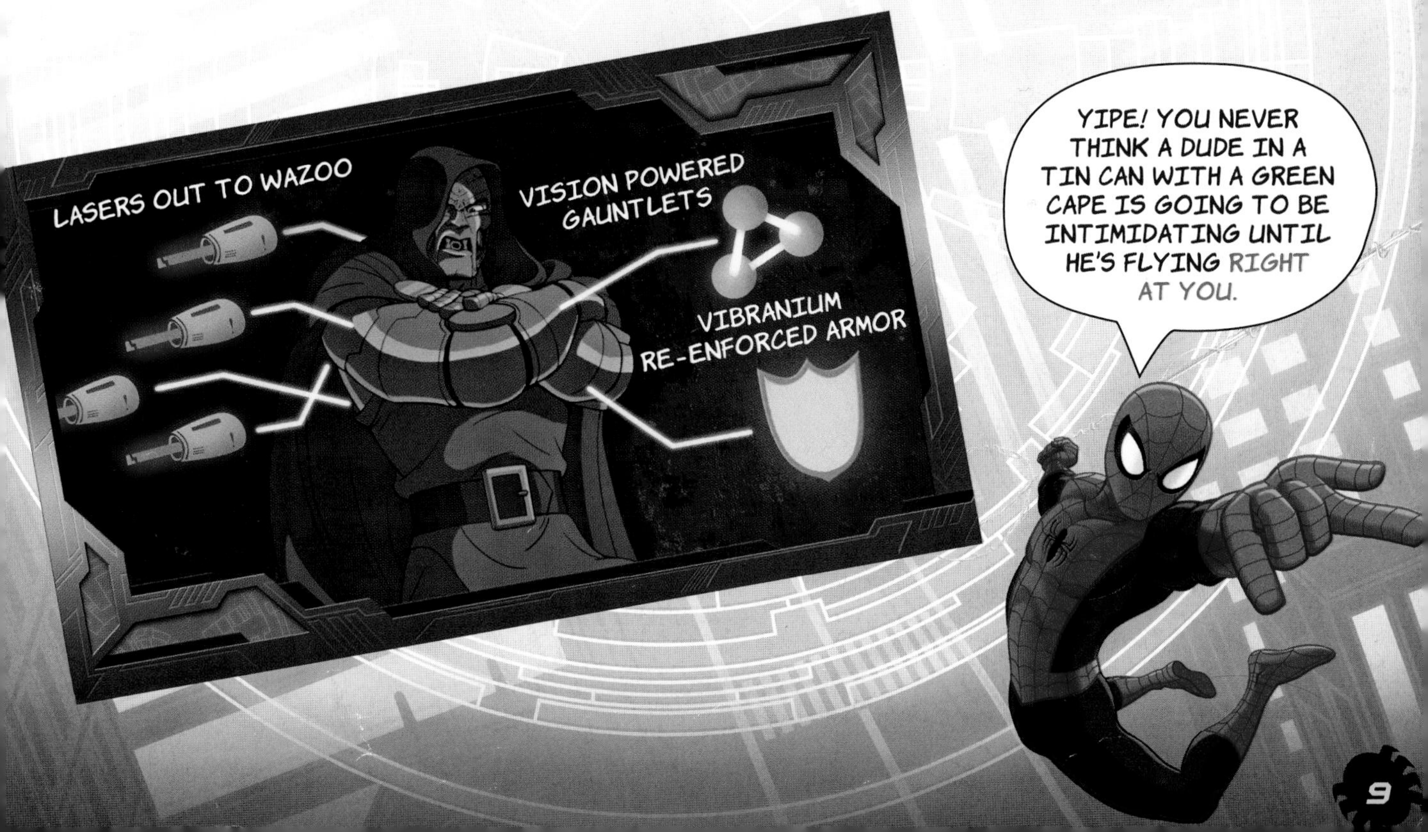
LASERS OUT TO WAZOO
VISION POWERED GAUNTLETS
VIBRANIUM RE-ENFORCED ARMOR
YIPE! YOU NEVER THINK A DUDE IN A TIN CAN WITH A GREEN CAPE IS GOING TO BE INTIMIDATING UNTIL HE'S FLYING RIGHT AT YOU.

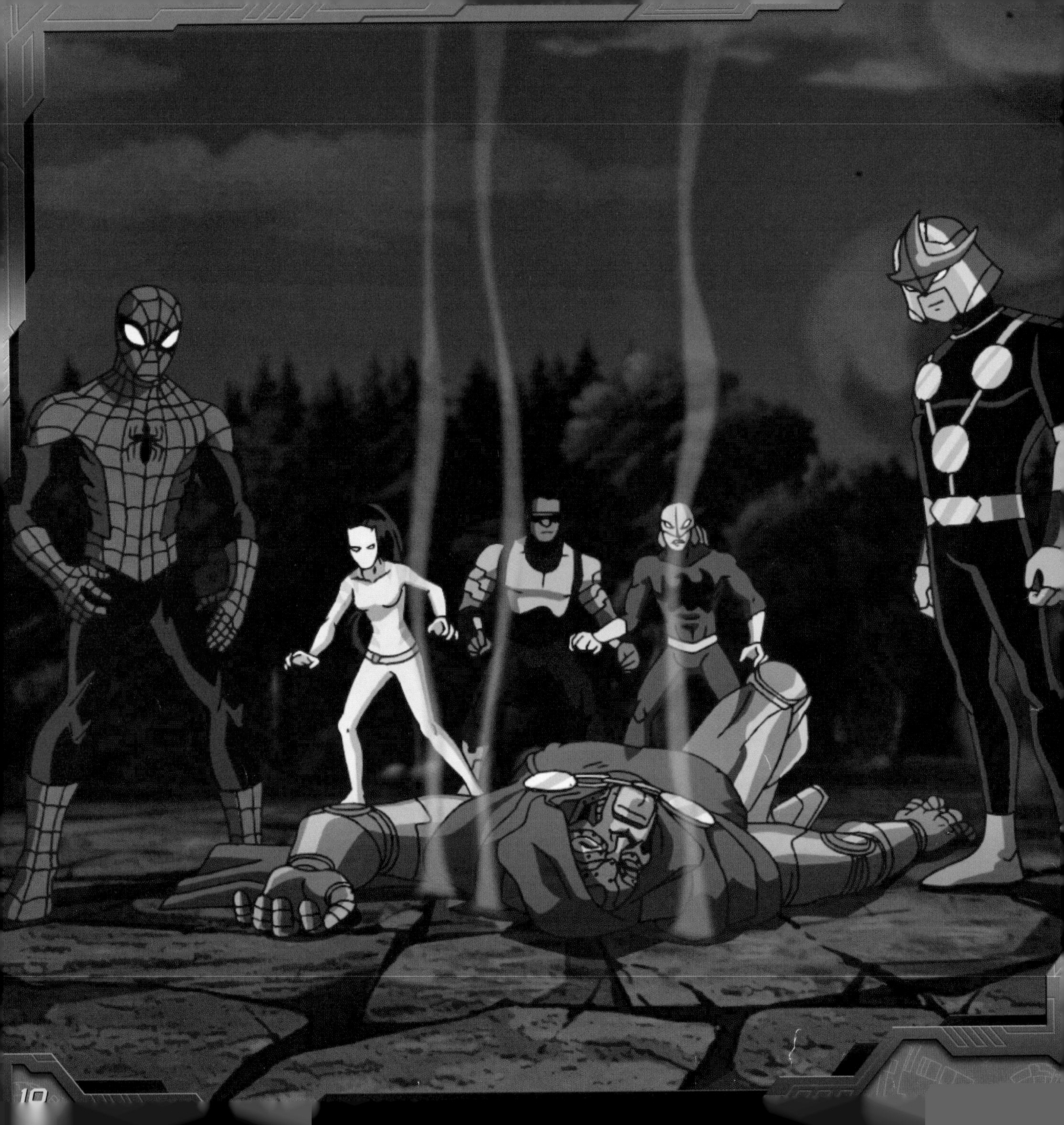

As Doom attacked, the team did their best to hold their ground and take him down. "I got this!" yelled Nova, flying straight at Doom. "No, I got this!" said Spidey, leaping into action. Amazingly, when the smoke cleared, Dr. Doom lay on the ground, defeated.

"Wow," said Nova, looking at Spider-Man. "I did it!"

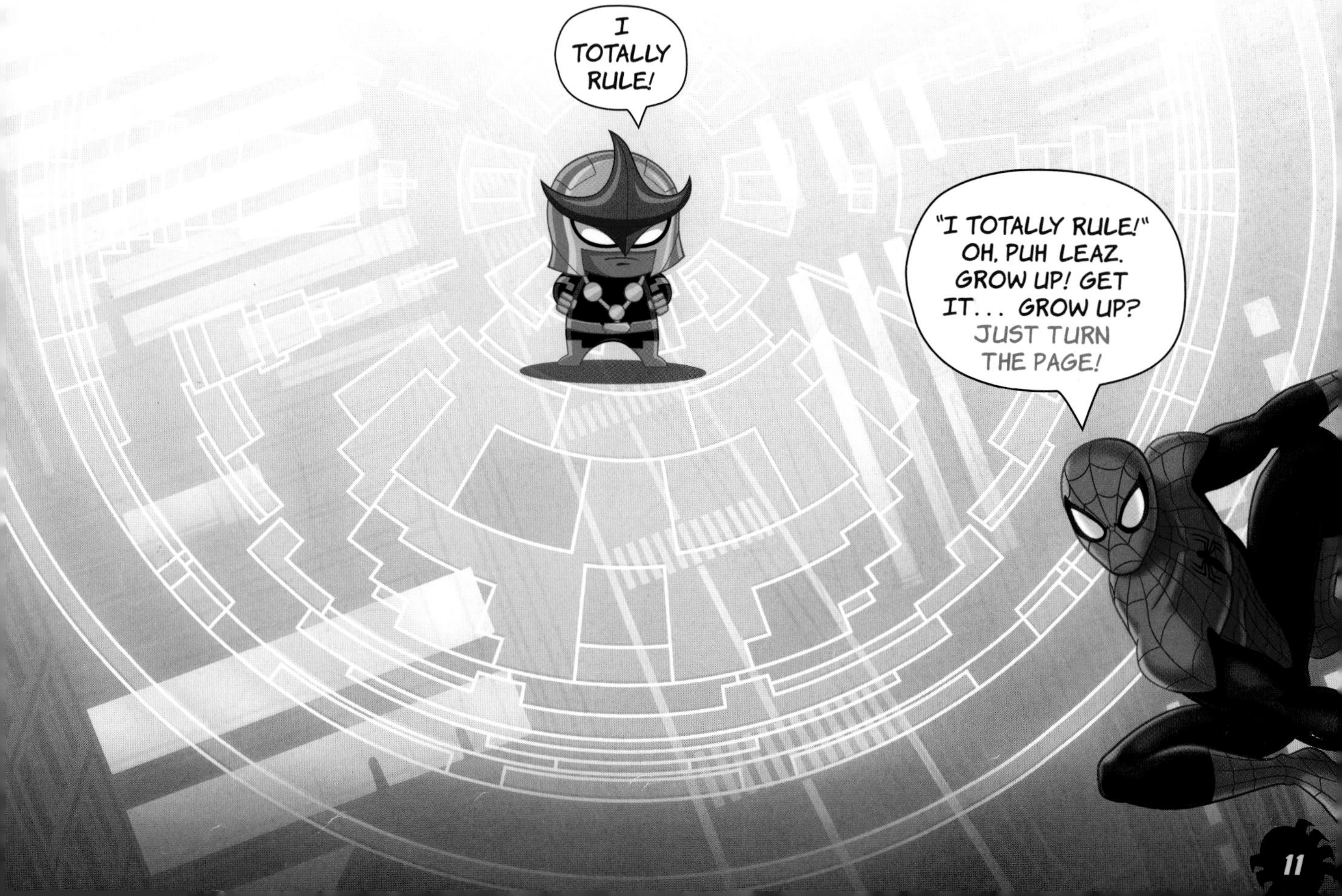
I TOTALLY RULE!
"I TOTALLY RULE!" OH, PUH LEAZ. GROW UP! GET IT... GROW UP? JUST TURN THE PAGE!

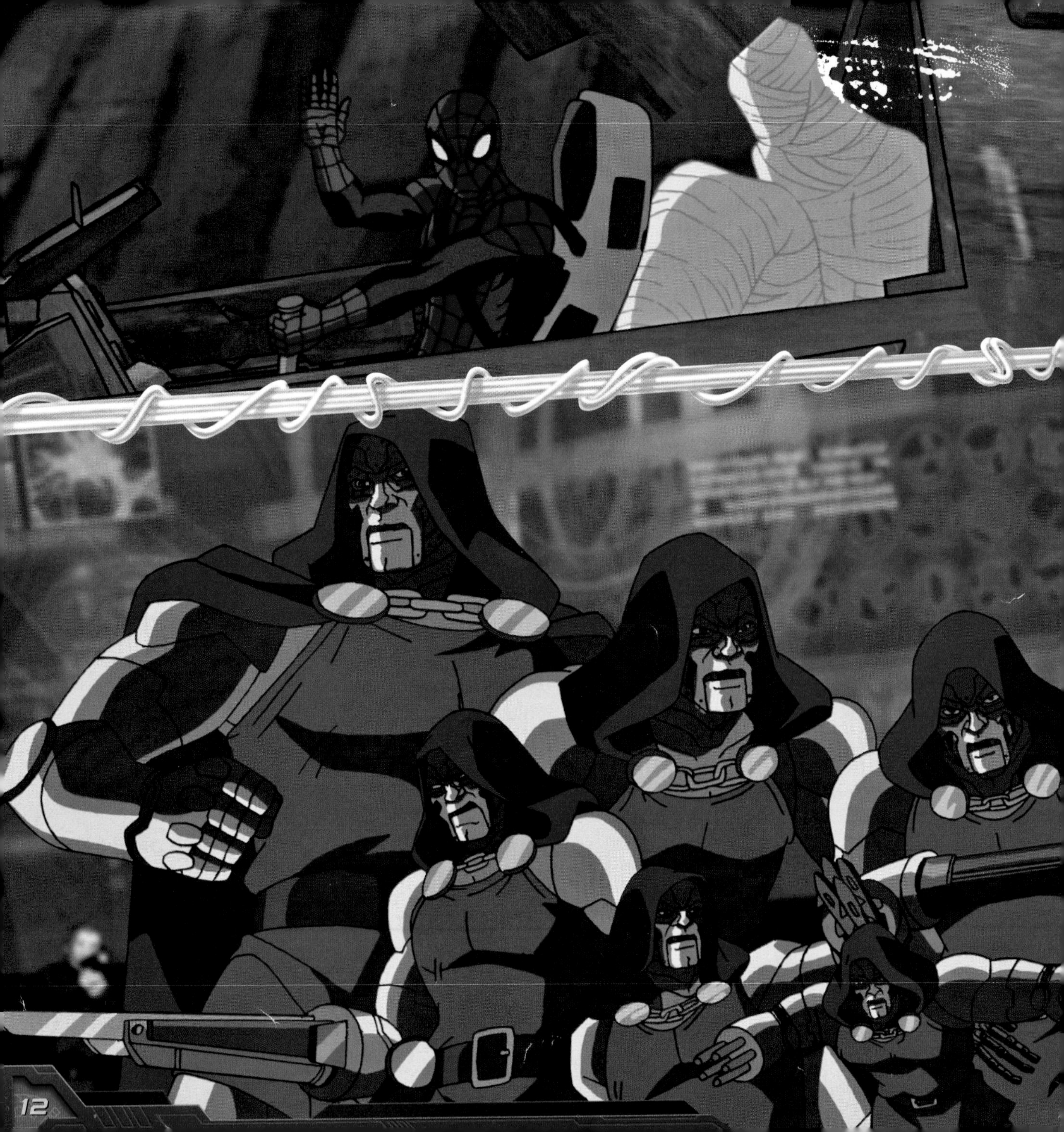

Before the team knew it, Spidey had Dr. Doom webbed up and in the back of the S.H.I.E.L.D. jet.

Back at the Helicarrier, Spider-Man and the team excitedly presented the web-wrapped form of Dr. Doom.

But there was something Spidey didn't know – it was a trap! The "Dr. Doom" they caught was actually a robot carrying other, smaller robots inside of it. Before they knew it, everyone was fighting a group of Doombots!

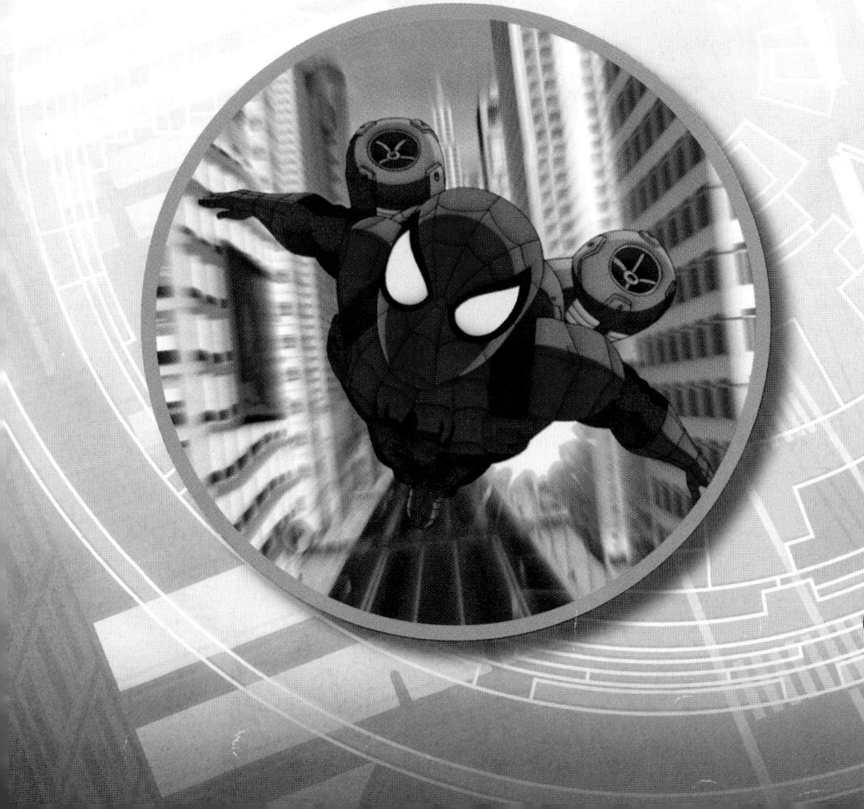

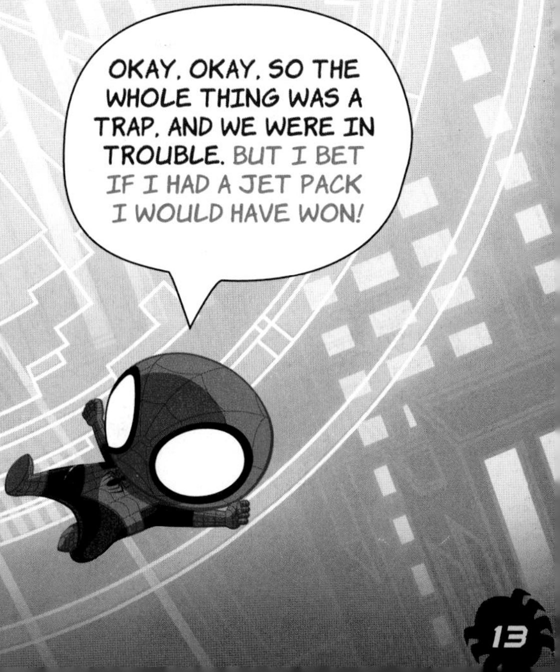
OKAY, OKAY, SO THE WHOLE THING WAS A TRAP, AND WE WERE IN TROUBLE. BUT I BET IF I HAD A JET PACK I WOULD HAVE WON!

"Split up and take them down before they reach the reactor!" ordered Fury. Spider-Man couldn't believe it! They had tried to prove their worth to Fury, and now things were worse than ever.

As the Doombots tore their way through the ship, the heroes tried to destroy them. Or at least catch them.

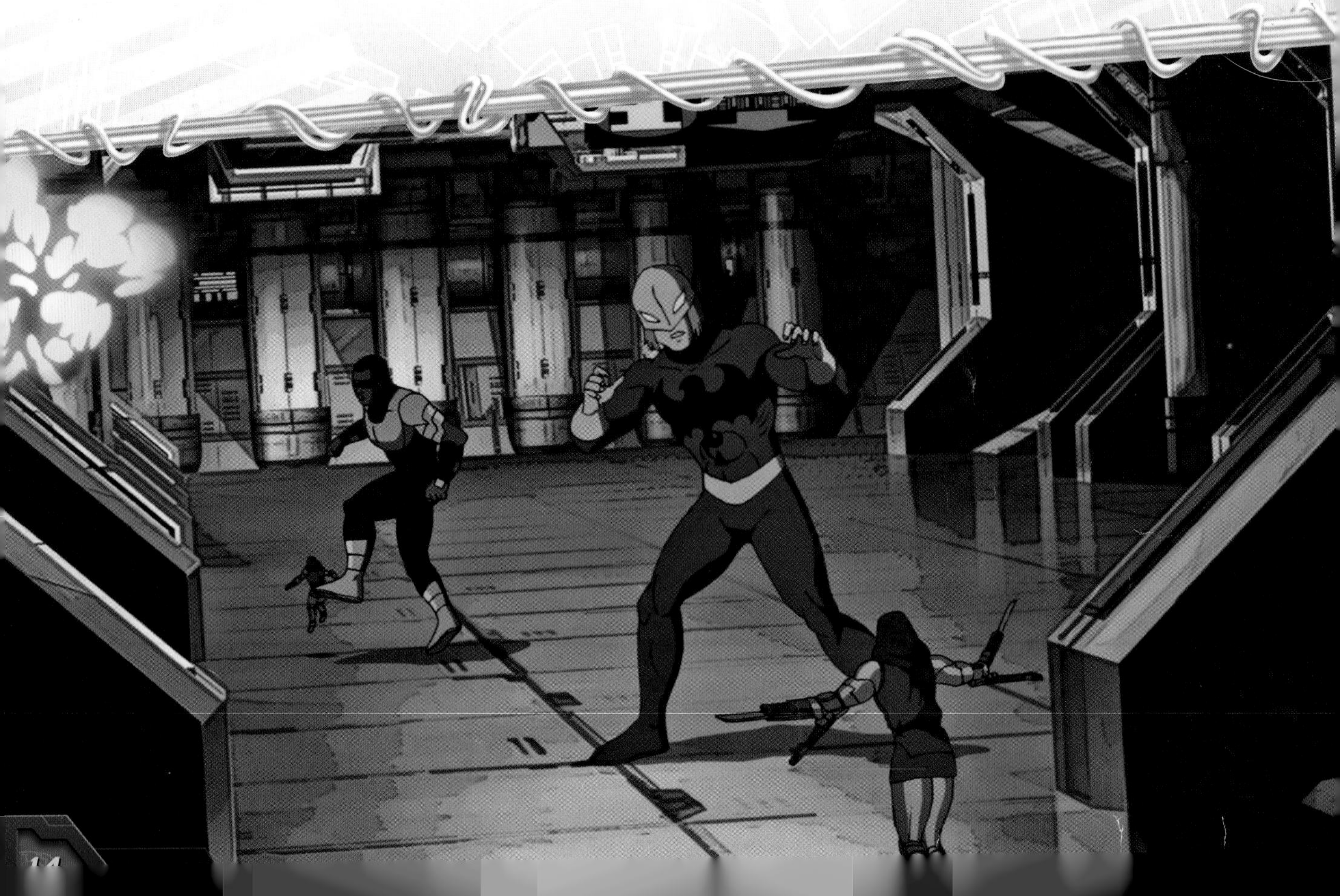

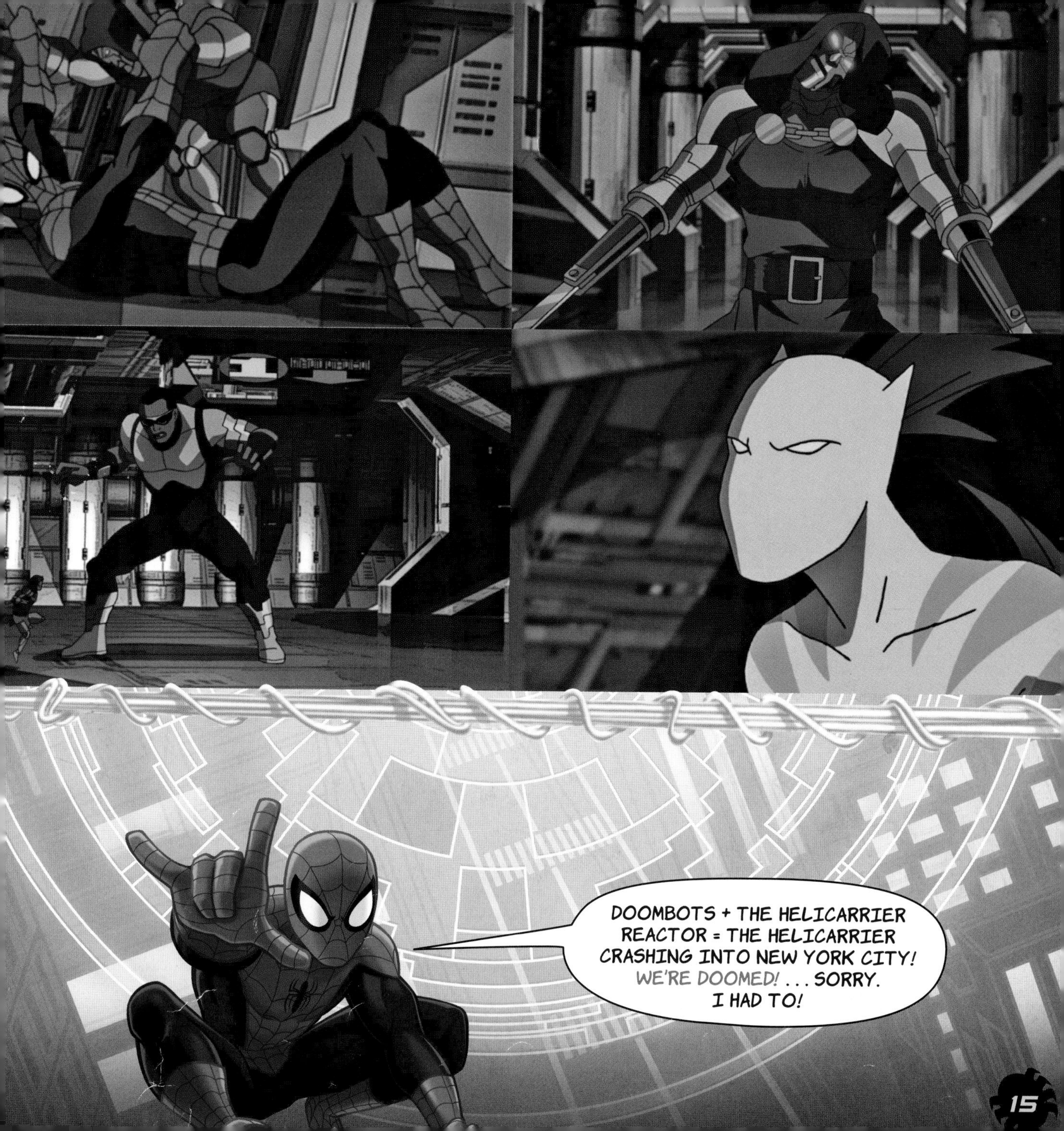
DOOMBOTS + THE HELICARRIER REACTOR = THE HELICARRIER CRASHING INTO NEW YORK CITY! WE'RE DOOMED! . . . SORRY. I HAD TO!

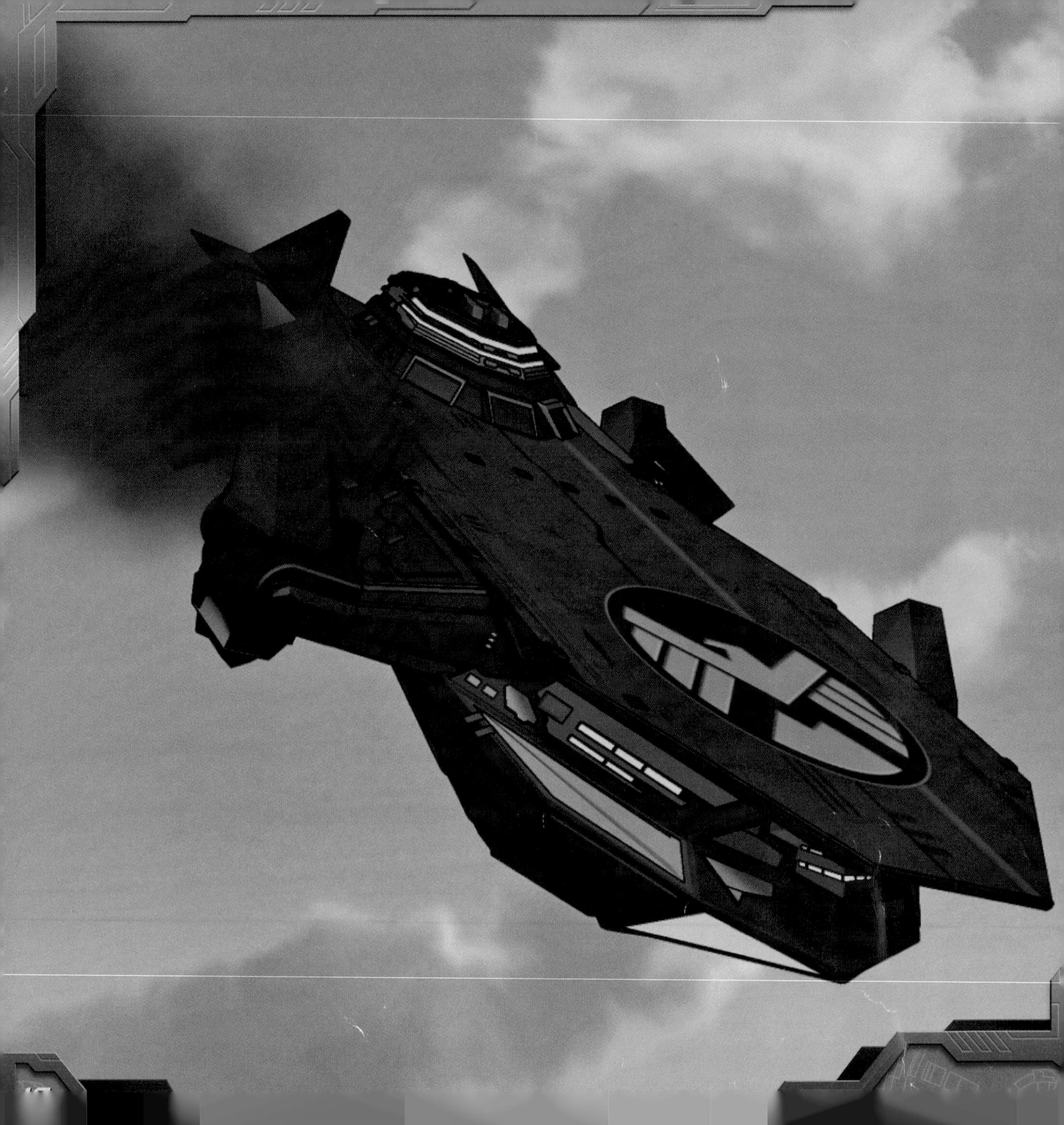

The Heroes were able to destroy a couple of the Doombots, but not before one of the engines was damaged. The Helicarrier was falling! Spider-Man turned to Nova and ordered him to get out and save the Helicarrier before it was too late!

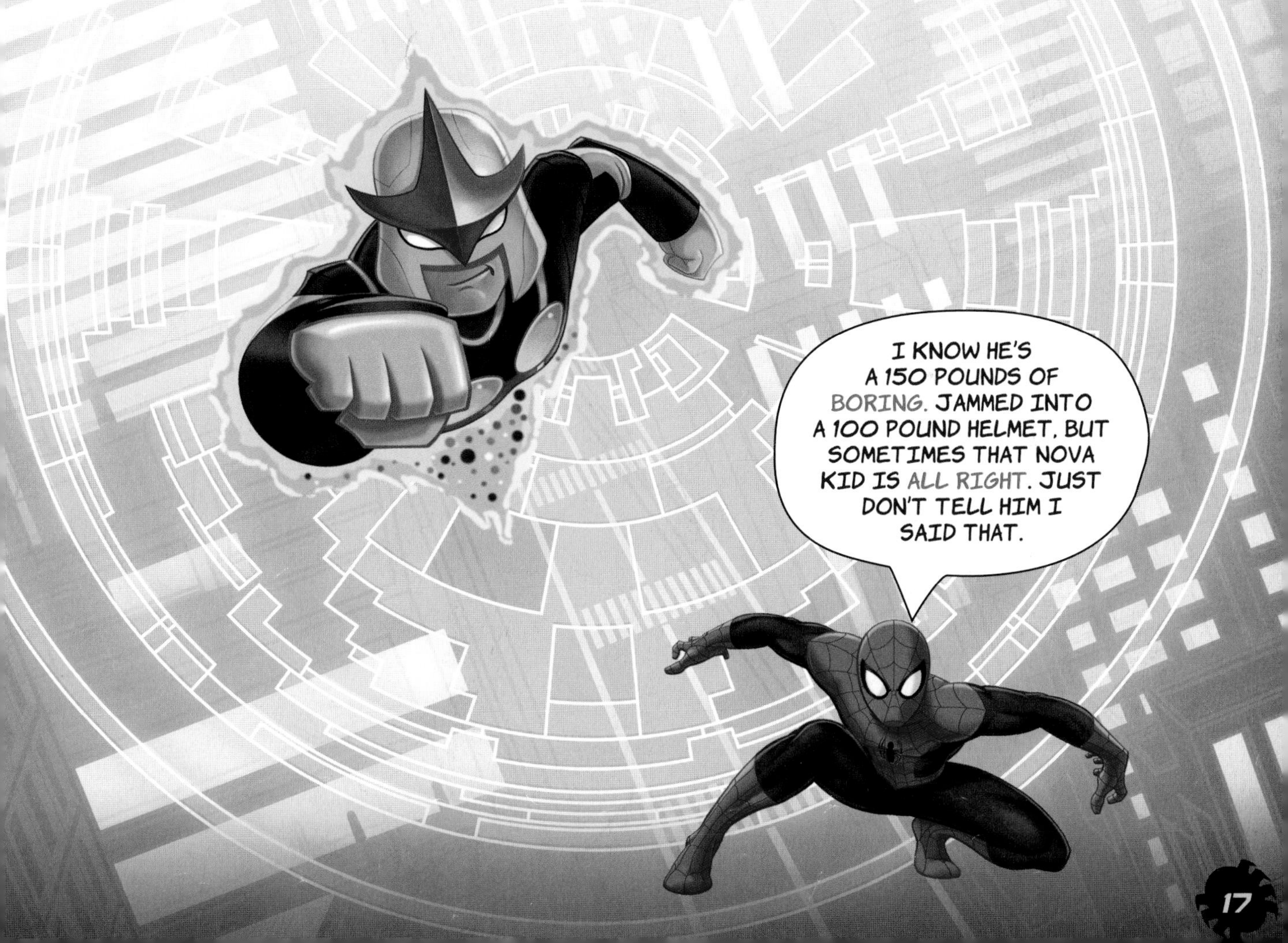
I KNOW HE'S A 150 POUNDS OF BORING. JAMMED INTO A 100 POUND HELMET, BUT SOMETIMES THAT NOVA KID IS ALL RIGHT. JUST DON'T TELL HIM I SAID THAT.

As Nova worked to stabilize the Helicarrier, the rest of the team rounded up the remaining Doombots. "I have a plan," said Spider-Man. "You have a death wish," said White Tiger.

"Quiet, you," Spidey demanded. "Okay, Iron Fist – I want you to punch a hole in the floor."

Iron Fist's super-powered blow broke through the steel-reinforced floors of the Helicarrier, and sent the team and the Doombots on a perilous freefall. "I don't think this was a very good plan," said White Tiger.

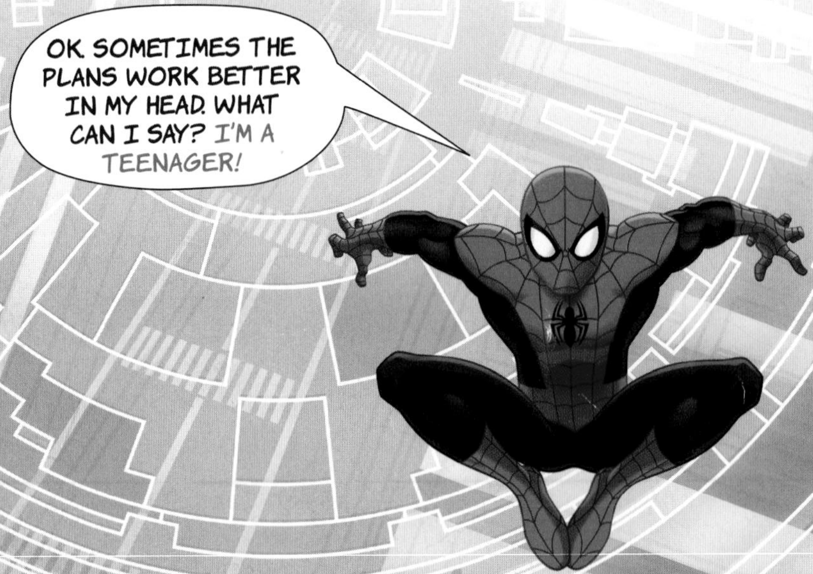
OK. SOMETIMES THE PLANS WORK BETTER IN MY HEAD. WHAT CAN I SAY? I'M A TEENAGER!

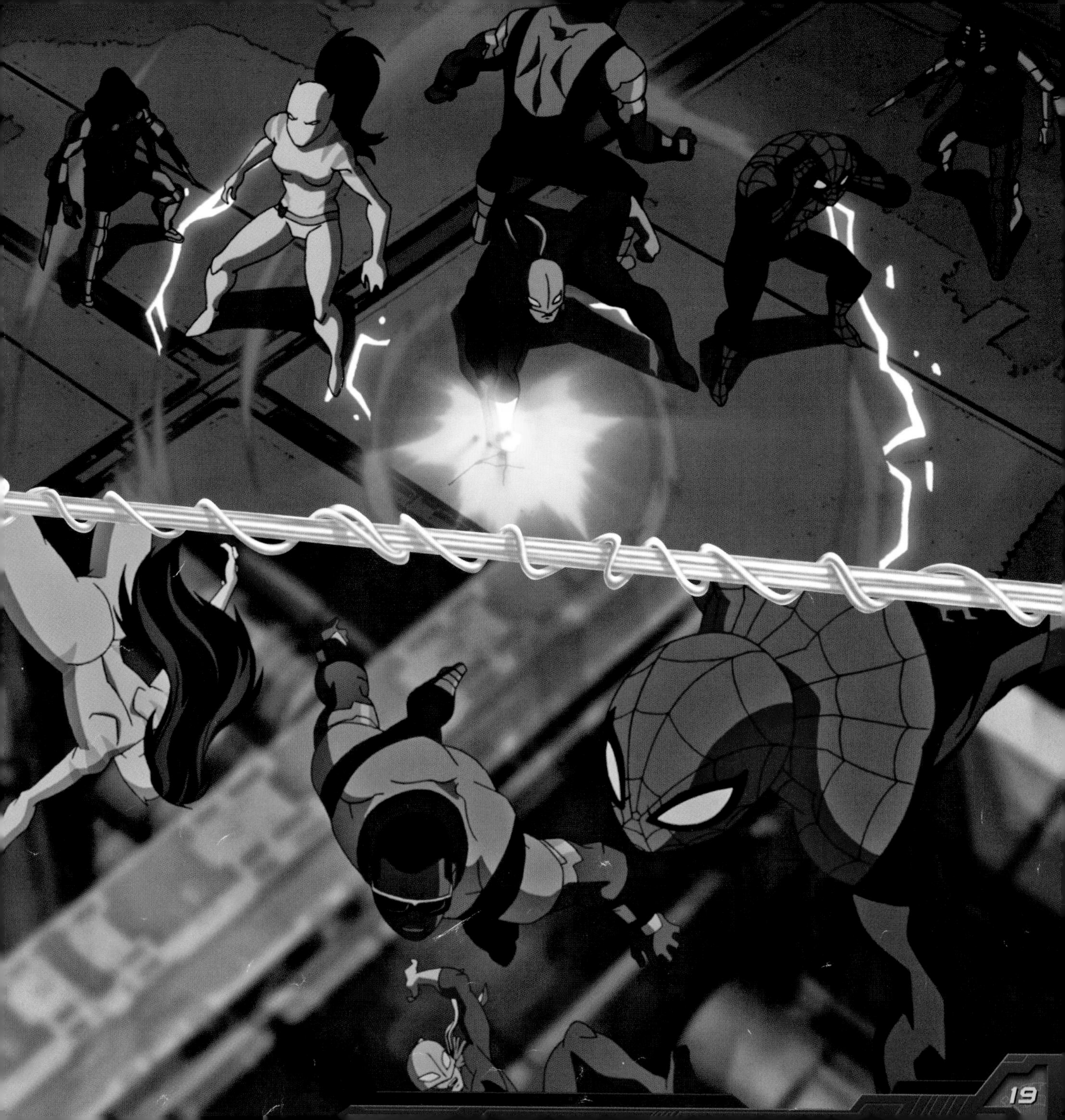

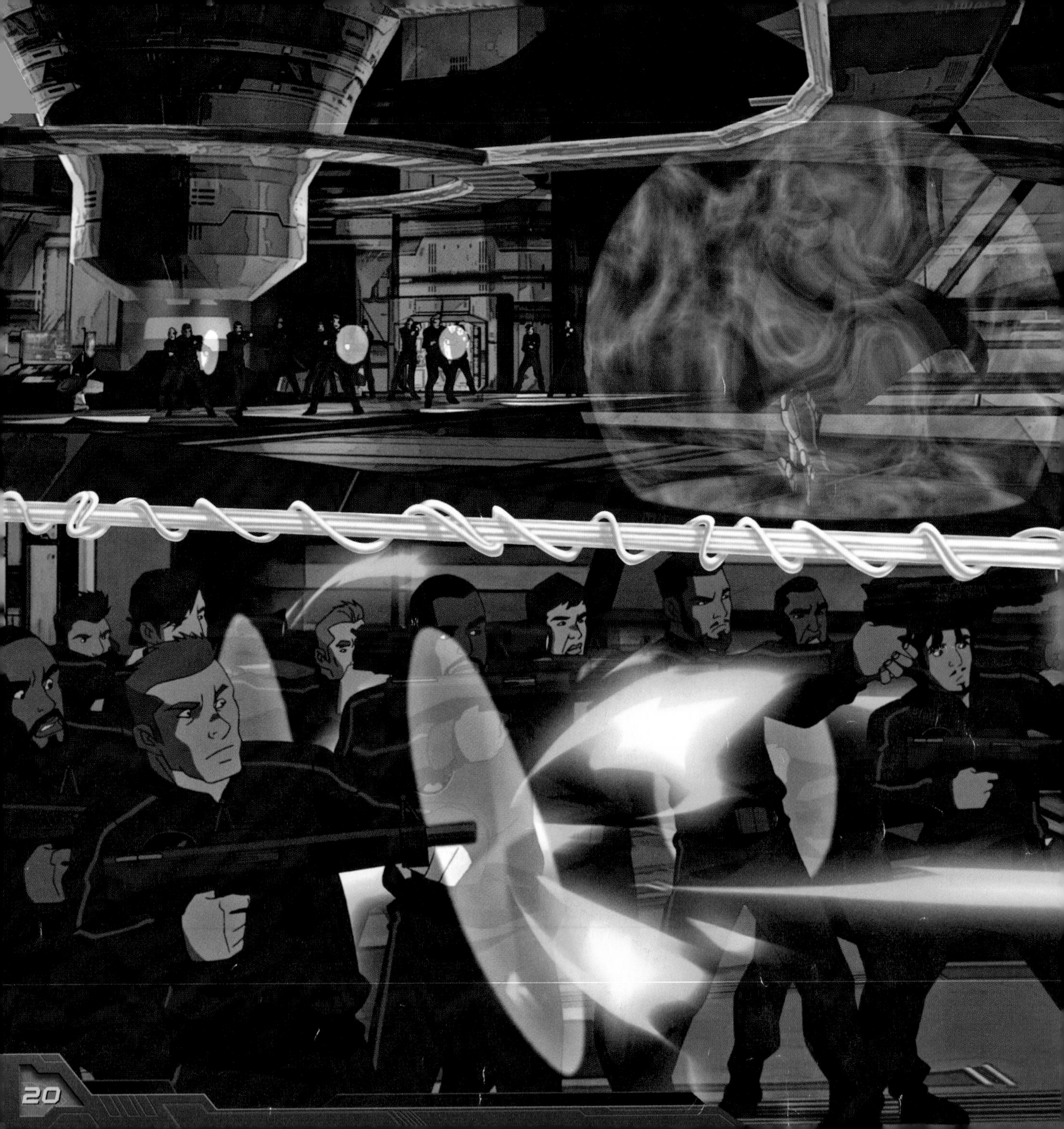

Nick Fury and the remaining S.H.I.E.L.D. agents were doing everything they could to keep the final Doombot away from the Helicarrier's power core.

Suddenly, there was an explosion from above! Fury looked up, and saw Spider-Man, White Tiger, Iron Fist, and Power Man, plummeting from the sky, surrounded by the other Doombots. Spider-Man shot a powerful webline, and the others grabbed onto him, swinging to safety.

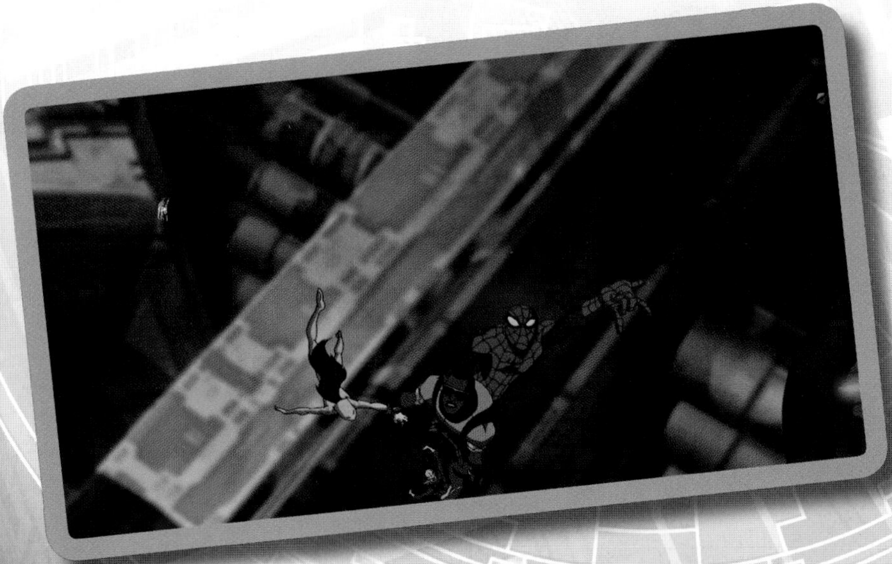

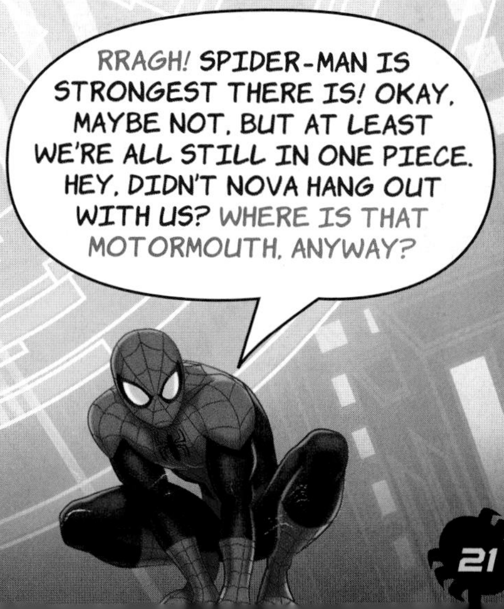
RRAGH! SPIDER-MAN IS STRONGEST THERE IS! OKAY, MAYBE NOT, BUT AT LEAST WE'RE ALL STILL IN ONE PIECE. HEY, DIDN'T NOVA HANG OUT WITH US? WHERE IS THAT MOTORMOUTH, ANYWAY?

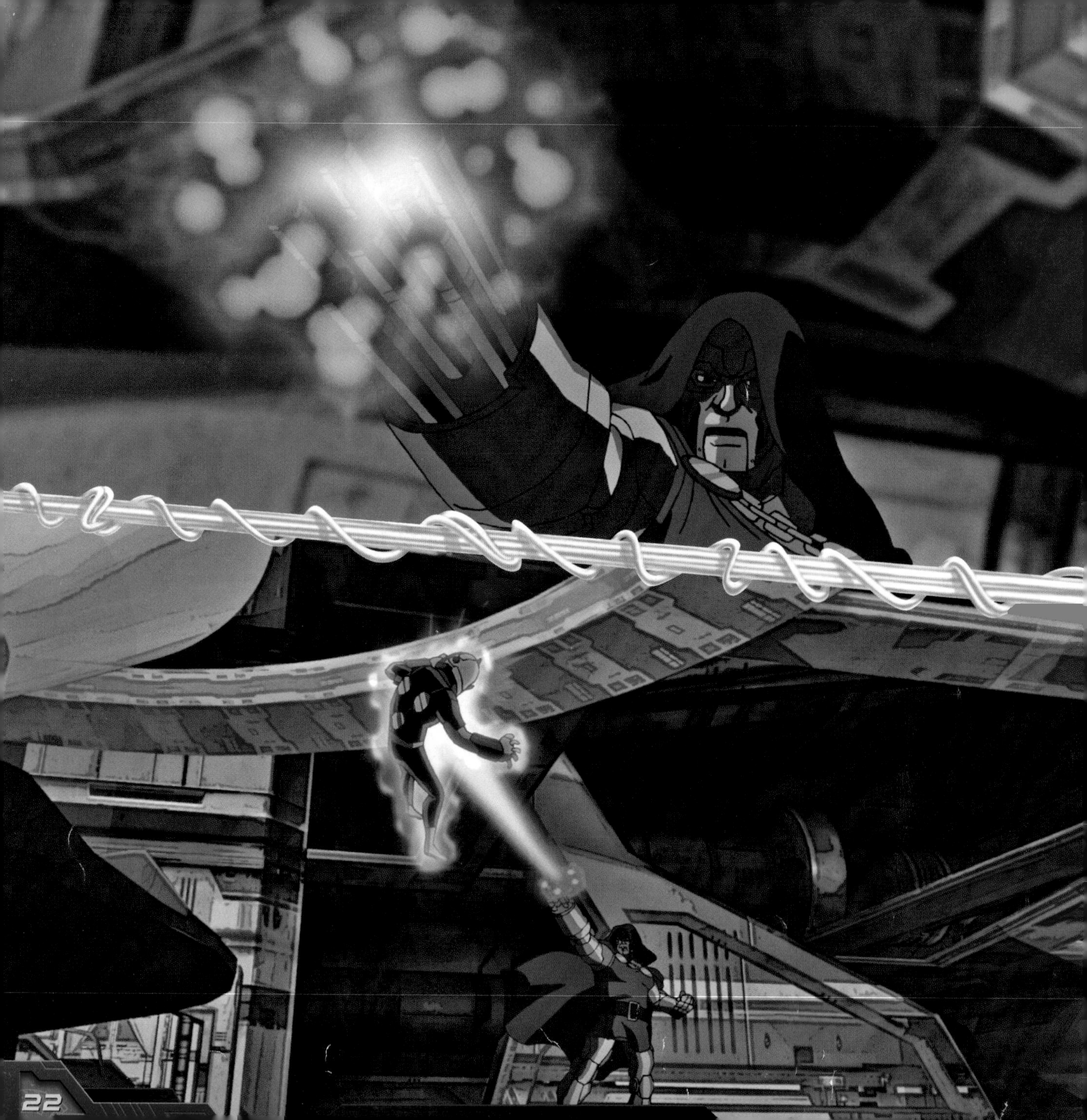

Across the room, the final Doombot powered-up. If it fired, the blast would destroy the entire Helicarrier! Just then, Nova streaked back into the room. "I got this!" he yelled, flying in front of the blast as the Doombot fired.

"Nova, no!!!" yelled Spider-Man.

The rest of the team jumped into action, and used their combined strength to take down the final Doombot. The day was saved! Just then, Nova's eyes opened and he got to his feet. "I didn't know you could absorb energy," Spidey said. "That's pretty sweet."

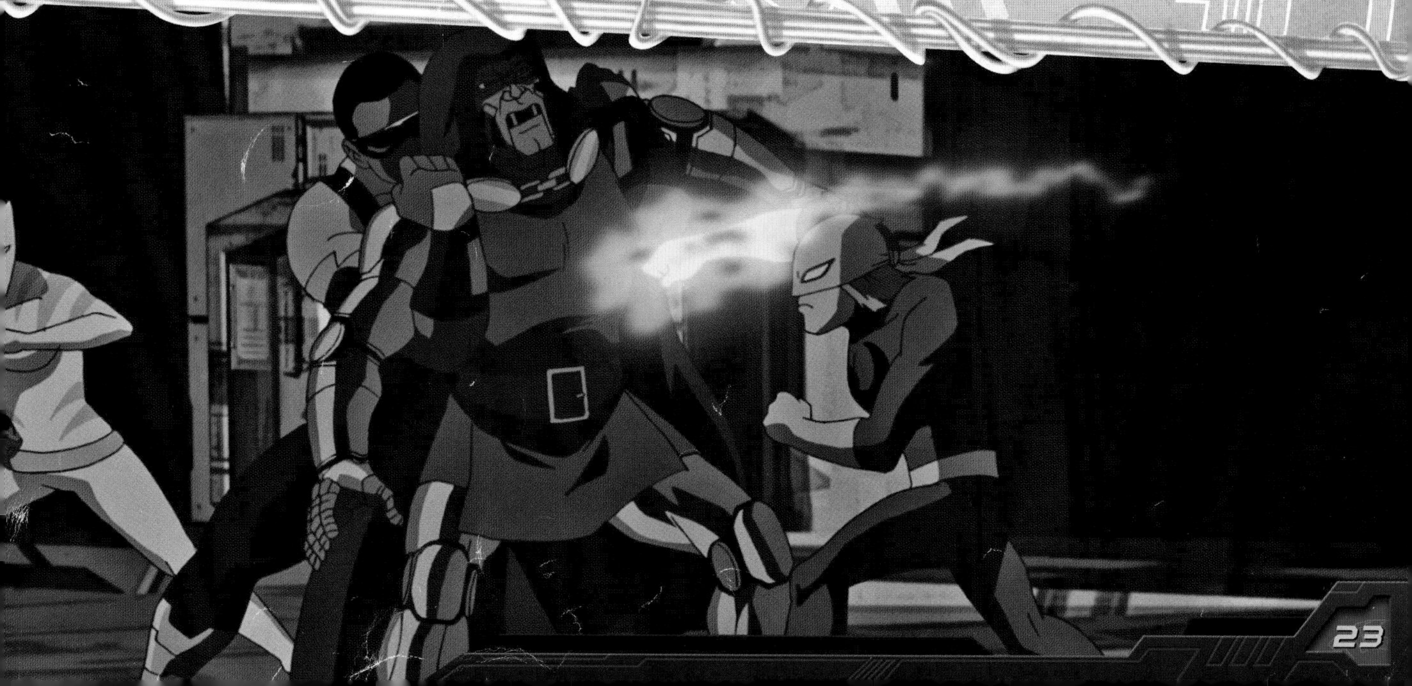

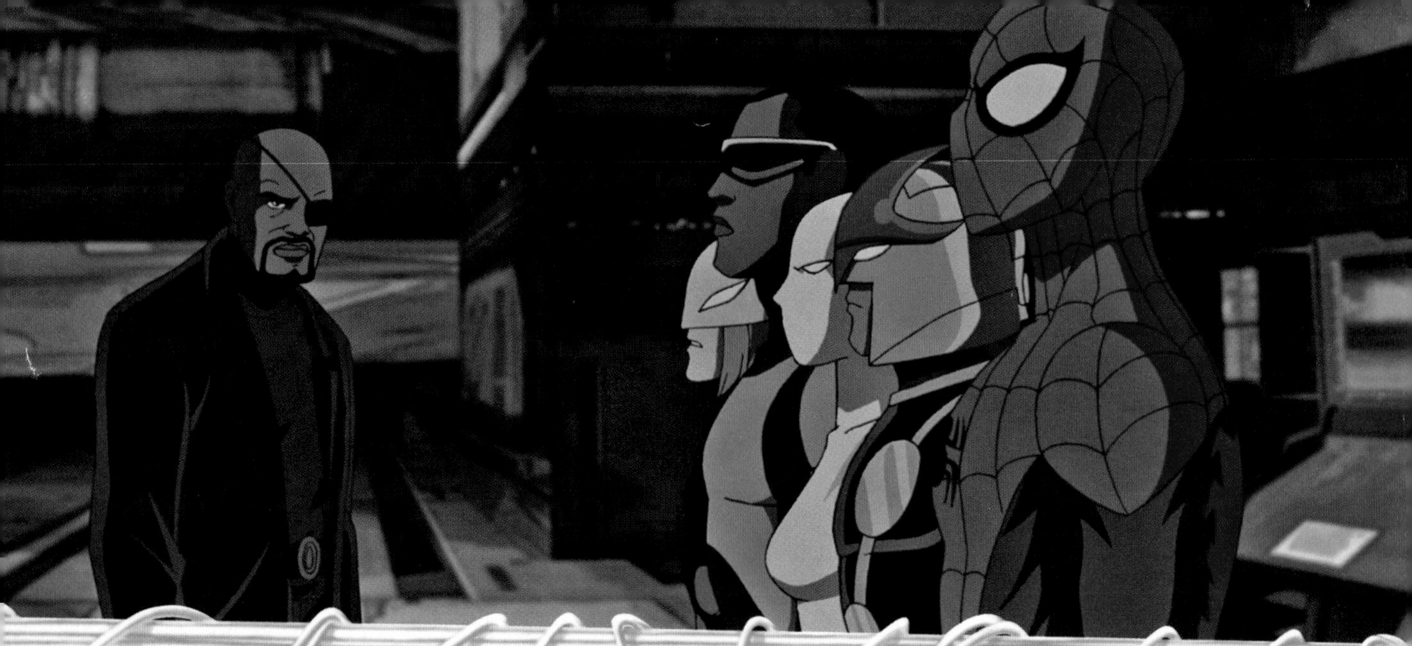

"Who's responsible for this?!?" Fury demanded. There was silence, then Spider-Man stepped forward.

"Sir, I apologize. I acted without thinking and endangered you, my team, and everyone in New York."

Suddenly, the rest of team moved forward. That's when Spidey realized being part of a group meant sticking by your teammates.

"We're all responsible for what happened today," said Nova.

Fury smiled. They had worked as a team and saved the day.

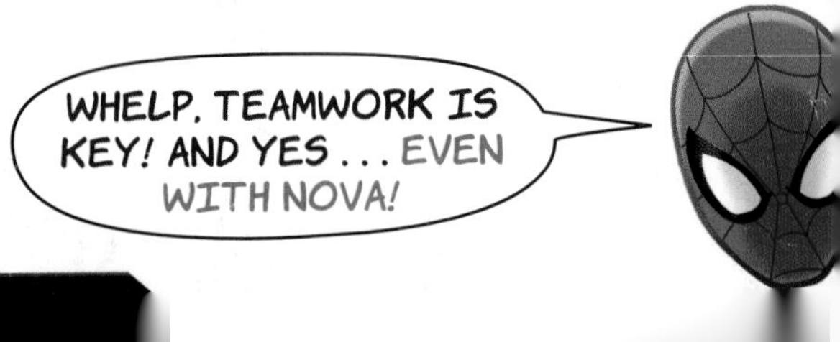
WHELP, TEAMWORK IS KEY! AND YES . . . EVEN WITH NOVA!